In the House
of the Seven Librarians

DATE DUE

Books by Ellen Klages

Fiction

White Sands, Red Menace
2008, Viking

Portable Childhoods
2007, Tachyon Publications

The Green Glass Sea
2006, Viking

Non-fiction

The Brain Explorer (with Pat Murphy, et al.)
1999, Henry Holt & Co.

Exploratorium: A Year of Discoveries
1997, Chronicle Books

The Science Explorer Out and About
(with Pat Murphy, et al.)
1997, Henry Holt & Co.

The Science Explorer (with Pat Murphy, et al.)
1996, Henry Holt & Co.

Harbin Hot Springs: Healing Waters, Sacred Land.
1991, HS Publishing, Inc.

Published by Aqueduct Press
PO Box 95787
Seattle, WA 98145-2787
www.aqueductpress.com

Copyright © 2012 by Ellen Klages
All rights reserved. First Printing, February 2012
10 9 8 7 6 5 4 3 2 1

First publication: *Firebirds Rising*, edited by Sharyn November.
Viking. April, 2006.

ISBN: 978-1-933500-98-0
Library of Congress Control Number: 2012931349
Cover illustration courtesy Anova Nurius

Library illustration acknowledgments, pg 79

Book Design by Kathryn Wilham

Printed in the USA by Applied Digital Imaging

In the House of the Seven Librarians

Ellen Klages

Berthoud Community Library District
Berthoud, CO

Once upon a time, the Carnegie Library sat on a wooded bluff on the east side of town: red brick and fieldstone, with turrets and broad windows facing the trees. Inside, green glass-shaded lamps cast warm yellow light onto oak tables ringed with spindle-backed chairs.

Books filled the dark shelves that stretched high up toward the pressed-tin ceiling. The floors were wood, except in the foyer, where they were pale beige marble. The loudest sounds were the ticking of the clock and the quiet, rhythmic *thwack* of a rubber stamp on a pasteboard card.

It was a cozy, orderly place.

Through twelve presidents and two world wars, the elms and maples grew tall outside the deep bay windows. Children leaped from *Peter Pan* to *Oliver Twist* and off to college, replaced at Story Hour by their younger brothers, cousins, daughters.

Then the library board—men in suits, serious men, men of money—met and cast their votes for progress. A new library, with fluorescent lights, much better for the children's eyes. Picture windows, automated systems, ergonomic plastic chairs. The town approved the levy, and the new library was built across town, convenient to the community center and the mall.

Some books were boxed and trundled down Broad Street, many others stamped DISCARD and left where they were, for a book sale in the fall. Interns from the university used the latest technology to transfer the cumbersome old card file and all the records onto floppy disks and microfiche. Progress, progress, progress.

The Ralph P. Mossberger Library (named after the local philanthropist and car dealer who had written the largest check) opened on a drizzly morning in late April. Everyone attended the ribbon-cutting ceremony and stayed for the speeches, because there would be cake after.

Everyone except the seven librarians from the Carnegie Library on the bluff across town.

Quietly, without a fuss (they were librarians, after all), while the town looked toward the future, they bought supplies: loose tea and English biscuits, packets of Bird's pudding and cans of beef-barley soup. They rearranged some of the shelves, brought in a few comfortable armchairs, nice china and teapots, a couch, towels for the shower, and some small braided rugs.

Then they locked the door behind them.

Each morning they woke and went about their chores. They shelved and stamped and cataloged, and in the evenings, every night, they read by lamplight.

Perhaps, for a while, some citizens remembered the old library, with the warm nostalgia of a favorite childhood toy that had disappeared one summer, never seen again. Others assumed it had been torn down long ago.

And so a year went by, then two, or perhaps a great many more. Inside, time had ceased to matter. Grass and brambles grew thick and tall around the fieldstone steps, and trees arched overhead as the forest folded itself around them like a cloak.

Inside, the seven librarians lived, quiet and content.

Until the day they found the baby.

Librarians are guardians of books. They guide others along their paths, offering keys to help unlock the doors of knowledge. But these seven had become a closed circle, no one to guide, no new minds to open onto worlds of possibility. They kept themselves busy, tidying orderly shelves and mending barely frayed bindings with stiff netting and glue, and began to bicker.

Ruth and Edith had been up half the night, arguing about whether or not subway tokens (of which there were half a dozen in the Lost and Found box) could be used to cast the *I Ching*. And so Blythe was on the stepstool in the 299s, reshelving the volume of hexagrams, when she heard the knock.

Odd, she thought. It's been some time since we've had visitors.

She tugged futilely at her shapeless cardigan as she clambered off the stool and trotted to the front door, where she stopped abruptly, her hand to her mouth in surprise.

A wicker basket, its contents covered with a red-checked cloth, as if for a picnic, lay in the wooden box beneath the Book Return chute. A small, cream-colored envelope poked out from one side.

"How nice!" Blythe said aloud, clapping her hands. She thought of fried chicken and potato salad—of which she was awfully fond— a Mason jar of lemonade, perhaps even a cherry pie? She lifted the basket by its round-arched handle. Heavy, for a picnic. But then, there *were* seven of them. Although Olive just ate like a bird, these days.

She turned and set it on top of the Circulation Desk, pulling the envelope free.

"What's *that*?" Marian asked, her lips in their accustomed moue of displeasure, as if the basket were an agent of chaos, existing solely to disrupt the tidy array of rubber stamps and file boxes that were her domain.

"A present," said Blythe. "I think it might be lunch."

Marian frowned. "For you?"

"I don't know yet. There's a note…" Blythe held up the envelope and peered at it. "No," she said. "It's addressed to 'The Librarians. Overdue Books Department.'"

"Well, that would be me," Marian said curtly. She was the youngest, and wore trouser suits with silk T-shirts. She had once been blond. She reached across the counter, plucked the envelope from Blythe's plump fingers, and sliced it open it with a filigreed brass stiletto.

"Hmph," she said after she'd scanned the contents.

"It *is* lunch, isn't it?" asked Blythe.

"Hardly." Marian began to read aloud:

> *This is overdue. Quite a bit, I'm afraid. I apologize. We moved to Topeka when I was very small, and Mother accidentally packed it up with the linens. I have traveled a long way to*

return it, and I know the fine must be large, but I have no money. As it is a book of fairy tales, I thought payment of a first-born child would be acceptable. I always loved the library. I'm sure she'll be happy there.

Blythe lifted the edge of the cloth. "Oh, my stars!"

A baby girl with a shock of wire-stiff black hair stared up at her, green eyes wide and curious. She was contentedly chewing on the corner of a blue book, half as big as she was. *Fairy Tales of the Brothers Grimm.*

"The Rackham illustrations," Blythe said as she eased the book away from the baby. "That's a lovely edition."

"But when was it checked out?" Marian demanded.

Blythe opened the cover and pulled the ruled card from the inside pocket. "October seventeenth, 1938," she said, shaking her head. "Goodness, at two cents a day, that's…" She shook her head again. Blythe had never been good with figures.

They made a crib for her in the bottom drawer of a file cabinet, displacing acquisition orders, zoning permits, and the instructions for the mimeograph, which they rarely used.

Ruth consulted Dr. Spock. Edith read Piaget. The two of them peered from text to infant and back again for a good long while before deciding that she was probably about nine months old. They sighed. Too young to read.

So they fed her cream and let her gum on biscuits, and each of the seven cooed and clucked and tickled her pink toes when they thought the others weren't looking. Harriet had been the oldest of nine girls, and knew more about babies than she really cared to. She washed and changed the diapers that had been tucked into the basket, and read *Goodnight Moon* and *Pat the Bunny* to the little girl, whom she called Polly—short for Polyhymnia, the muse of oratory and sacred song.

Blythe called her Bitsy, and Li'l Precious.

Marian called her "the foundling," or "That Child You Took In," but did her share of cooing and clucking, just the same.

When the child began to walk, Dorothy blocked the staircase with stacks of Comptons, which she felt was an inferior encyclopedia, and let her pull herself up on the bottom drawers of the card catalog. Anyone looking up Zithers or Zippers (see *Slide Fasteners*) soon found many of the cards fused together with grape jam. When she began to talk, they made a little bed nook next to the fireplace in the Children's Room.

It was high time for Olive to begin the child's education.

Olive had been the children's librarian since before recorded time, or so it seemed. No one knew how old she was, but she vaguely remembered waving to President Coolidge. She still had all of her marbles, though every one of them was a bit odd and rolled asymmetrically.

She slept on a daybed behind a reference shelf that held *My First Encyclopedia* and *The Wonder Book of Trees,* among others. Across the room, the child's first "big-girl bed" was yellow, with decals of a fairy and a horse on the headboard, and a rocket ship at the foot, because they weren't sure about her preferences.

At the beginning of her career, Olive had been an ordinary-sized librarian, but by the time she began the child's lessons, she was not much taller than her toddling charge. Not from osteoporosis or dowager's hump or other old-lady maladies, but because she had tired of stooping over tiny chairs and bending to knee-high shelves. She had been a grown-*up* for so long that when the library closed, she had decided it was time to grow *down* again, and was finding that much more comfortable.

She had a remarkably cozy lap for a woman her size.

The child quickly learned her alphabet, all the shapes and colors, the names of zoo animals, and fourteen different kinds of dinosaurs, all of whom were dead.

By the time she was four, or thereabouts, she could sound out the letters for simple words — *cup* and *lamp* and *stairs*. And that's how she came to name herself.

Olive had fallen asleep over *Make Way for Ducklings,* and all the other librarians were busy somewhere else. The child was bored. She tiptoed out of the Children's Room, hugging the shadows of the walls and shelves, crawling by the base of the Circulation Desk so that Marian wouldn't see her, and made her way to the alcove that held the Card Catalog.

The heart of the library. Her favorite, most forbidden place to play.

Usually she crawled underneath and tucked herself into the corner formed of oak cabinet, marble floor, and plaster walls. It was a fine place to play Hide-and-Seek, even if it was mostly just Hide. The corner was a cave, a bunk on a pirate ship, a cupboard in a magic wardrobe.

But that afternoon she looked at the white cards on the fronts of the drawers, and her eyes widened in recognition. Letters! In her very own alphabet. Did they spell words? Maybe the drawers were all *full* of words, a huge wooden box of words. The idea almost made her dizzy.

She walked to the other end of the cabinet and looked up, tilting her neck back until it crackled. Four drawers from top to bottom. Five drawers across. She sighed. She was only tall enough to reach the bottom row of drawers. She traced a gentle finger around the little brass frames, then very carefully pulled out the white cards inside and laid them on the floor in a neat row:

She squatted over them, her tongue sticking out of the corner of her mouth in concentration, and tried to read.

"Sound it out." She could almost hear Olive's voice, soft and patient. She took a deep breath.

"Duh-in-s—" and then she stopped, because the last card had too many letters, and she didn't know any words that had Xs in them. Well, xylophone. But the X was in the front, and that wasn't the same. She tried anyway. "Duh-ins-zzzigh," and frowned.

She squatted lower, so low she could feel cold marble under her cotton pants, and put her hand on top of the last card. One finger covered the X and her pinkie covered the Z (another letter that was useless for spelling ordinary things). That left *Y*. *Y* at the end was good. funn*Y*. happ*Y*.

"Duh-ins-see," she said slowly. "Dinsy."

That felt very good to say, hard and soft sounds and hissing *S*s mixing in her mouth, so she said it again, louder, which made her laugh, so she said it again, very loud: "DINSY!"

There is nothing quite like a loud voice in a library to get a lot of attention very fast. Within a minute, all seven of the librarians stood in the doorway of the alcove.

"What on earth?" said Harriet.

"*Now* what have you…" said Marian.

"What have you spelled, dear?" asked Olive in her soft little voice.

"I made it myself," the girl replied.

"Just gibberish," murmured Edith, though not unkindly. "It doesn't mean a thing."

The child shook her head. "Does so. Olive," she said, pointing to Olive. "Do'thy, Edith, Harwiet, Bithe, Ruth." She paused and rolled her eyes. "Mawian," she added, a little less cheerfully. Then she pointed to herself. "And Dinsy."

"Oh, now, Polly," said Harriet.

"Dinsy," said Dinsy.

"Bitsy?" Blythe tried hopefully.

"*Din*sy," said Dinsy.

And that was that.

At three every afternoon, Dinsy and Olive made a two-person circle on the braided rug in front of the bay window, and had Story Time. Sometimes Olive read aloud from *Beezus and Ramona* and *Half Magic,* and sometimes Dinsy read to Olive: *The King's Stilts,* and *In the Night Kitchen,* and *Winnie-the-Pooh.* Dinsy liked that one especially, and took it to bed with her so many times that Edith had to repair the binding. Twice.

That was when Dinsy first wished upon the Library.

A note about the Library:

Knowledge is not static; information must flow in order to live. Every so often one of the librarians would discover a new addition. *Harry Potter and the Sorcerer's Stone* appeared one rainy afternoon, Rowling shelved neatly between Rodgers and Saint-Exupéry, as if it had always been there. Blythe found a book of Thich

Nhat Hanh's writings in the 294s one day while she was dusting, and Feynman's lectures on physics showed up on Dorothy's shelving cart after she'd gone to make a cup of tea.

It didn't happen often; the Library was selective about what it chose to add, rejecting flash-in-the-pan best-sellers, sifting for the long haul, looking for those voices that would stand the test of time next to Dickens and Tolkien, Woolf and Gould.

The librarians took care of the books, and the Library watched over them in return. It occasionally left treats: a bowl of ripe tangerines on the Formica counter of the Common Room; a gold foil box of chocolate creams; seven small, stemmed glasses of sherry on the table one teatime. Their biscuit tin remained full, the cream in the Wedgwood jug stayed fresh, and the ink pad didn't dry out. Even the little pencils stayed needle sharp, never whittling down to finger-cramping nubs.

Some days the Library even hid Dinsy, when she had made a mess and didn't want to be found, or when one of the librarians was in a dark mood. It rearranged itself, just a bit, so that in her wanderings she would find a new alcove or cubbyhole, and once a secret passage that led to a previously unknown balcony overlooking the Reading Room. When she went back a week later, she found only blank wall.

And so it was, one night when she was sixish, that Dinsy first asked the Library for a boon. Lying in her tiny yellow bed, the fraying *Pooh* under her pillow, she wished for a bear to cuddle. Books were small comfort once the lights were out, and their hard, sharp corners made them awkward companions under the covers. She lay with one arm crooked around a soft, imaginary bear, and wished and wished until her eyelids fluttered into sleep.

The next morning, while they were all having tea and toast with jam, Blythe came into the Common Room with a quizzical look on her face and her hands behind her back.

"The strangest thing," she said. "On my way up here I glanced over at the Lost and Found. Couldn't tell you why. Nothing lost in ages. But this must have caught my eye."

She held out a small brown bear, one shoebutton eye missing, bits of fur gone from its belly, as if it had been loved almost to pieces.

"It seems to be yours," she said with a smile, turning up one padded foot, where DINSY was written in faded laundry-marker black.

Dinsy wrapped her whole self around the cotton-stuffed body and skipped for the rest of the morning. Later, after Olive gave her a snack—cocoa and a Lorna Doone—Dinsy cupped her hand and blew a kiss to the oak woodwork.

"Thank you," she whispered, and put half her cookie in a crack between two tiles on the Children's Room fireplace when Olive wasn't looking.

Dinsy and Olive had a lovely time. One week they were pirates, raiding the Common Room for booty (and raisins). The next they were princesses, trapped in the turret with *At the Back of the North Wind,* and the week after that they were knights in shining armor, rescuing damsels in distress, a game Dinsy especially savored because it annoyed Marian to be rescued.

But the year she turned seven-and-a-half, Dinsy stopped reading stories. Quite abruptly, on an afternoon that Olive said later had really *felt* like a Thursday.

"Stories are for babies," Dinsy said. "I want to read about *real* people." Olive smiled a sad smile and pointed toward the far wall, because Dinsy was not the first child to make that same pronouncement, and she had known this phase would come.

After that, Dinsy devoured biographies, starting with the orange ones, the Childhoods of Famous Americans: *Thomas Edison, Young Inventor.* She worked her way from Abigail Adams to John Peter Zenger, all along the west side of the Children's Room, until one day she went around the corner, where Science and History began.

She stood in the doorway, looking at the rows of grown-up books, when she felt Olive's hand on her shoulder.

"Do you think maybe it's time you moved across the hall?" Olive asked softly.

Dinsy bit her lip, then nodded. "I can come back to visit, can't I? When I want to read stories again?"

"For as long as you like, dear. Anytime at all."

So Dorothy came and gathered up the bear and the pillow and the yellow toothbrush. Dinsy kissed Olive on her papery cheek and, holding Blythe's hand, moved across the hall, to the room where all the books had numbers.

Blythe was plump and freckled and frizzled. She always looked a little flushed, as if she had just that moment dropped what she was doing to rush over and greet you. She wore rumpled tweed skirts and a shapeless cardigan whose original color was impossible to guess. She had bright, dark eyes like a spaniel's, which Dinsy thought was appropriate, because Blythe *lived* to fetch books. She wore a locket with a small rotogravure picture of Melvil Dewey and kept a variety of sweets—sour balls and mints and Necco wafers—in her desk drawer.

Dinsy had always liked her.

She was not as sure about Dorothy.

Over *her* desk, Dorothy had a small, framed medal on a royal-blue ribbon, won for "Excellence in Classification Studies." She could operate the ancient black Remington typewriter with brisk efficiency, and even, on occasion, coax chalky gray prints out of the wheezing old copy machine.

She was a tall, rawboned woman with steely blue eyes, good posture, and even better penmanship. Dinsy was a little frightened of her, at first, because she seemed so stern, and because she looked like magazine pictures of the Wicked Witch of the West, or at least Margaret Hamilton.

But that didn't last long.

"You should be very careful not to slip on the floor in here," Dorothy said on their first morning. "Do you know why?"

Dinsy shook her head.

"Because now you're in the non*friction* room!" Dorothy's angular face cracked into a wide grin.

Dinsy groaned. "Okay," she said after a minute. "How do you file marshmallows?"

Dorothy cocked her head. "Shoot."

"By the *Gooey* Decimal System!"

Dinsy heard Blythe tsk-tsk, but Dorothy laughed out loud, and from then on they were fast friends.

The three of them used the large, sunny room as an arena for endless games of I Spy and Twenty Questions as Dinsy learned her way around the shelves. In the evenings, after supper, they played Authors and Scrabble, and (once) tried to keep a running rummy score in Base Eight.

Dinsy sat at the court of Napoleon, roamed the jungles near Timbuktu, and was a frequent guest at the Round Table. She knew all the kings of England and the difference between a pergola and a folly. She knew the names of 112 breeds of sheep, and loved to say "Barbados Blackbelly" over and over, although it was difficult to work into conversations. When she affectionately, if misguidedly, referred to Blythe as a "Persian Fat-Rumped," she was sent to bed without supper.

A note about time:

Time had become quite flexible inside the library. (This is true of most places with interesting books. Sit down to read for twenty minutes, and suddenly it's dark, with no clue as to where the hours have gone.)

As a consequence, no one was really sure about the day of the week, and there was frequent disagreement about the month and year. As the keeper of the date stamp at the front desk, Marian was the arbiter of such things. But she often had a cocktail after dinner, and many mornings she couldn't recall if she'd already turned the little wheel, or how often it had slipped her mind, so she frequently set it a day or two ahead—or back three—just to make up.

One afternoon, on a visit to Olive and the Children's Room, Dinsy looked up from *Little Town on the Prairie* and said, "When's my birthday?"

Olive thought for a moment. Because of the irregularities of time, holidays were celebrated a bit haphazardly. "I'm not sure, dear. Why do you ask?"

"Laura's going to a birthday party, in this book," she said, holding it up. "And it's fun. So I thought maybe I could have one."

"I think that would be lovely," Olive agreed. "We'll talk to the others at supper."

"Your birthday?" said Harriet as she set the table a few hours later. "Let me see." She began to count on her fingers. "You arrived in April, according to Marian's stamp, and you were about nine months old, so—" She pursed her lips as she ticked off the months. "You must have been born in July!"

"But when's my birth*day*?" Dinsy asked impatiently.

"Not sure," said Edith as she ladled out the soup.

"No way to tell," Olive agreed.

"How does July fifth sound?" offered Blythe, as if it were a point of order to be voted on. Blythe counted best by fives.

"Fourth," said Dorothy. "Independence Day. Easy to remember?"

Dinsy shrugged. "Okay." It hadn't seemed so complicated in the Little House book. "When is that? Is it soon?"

"Probably." Ruth nodded.

A few weeks later, the librarians threw her a birthday party.

Harriet baked a spice cake with pink frosting, and wrote DINSY on top in red licorice laces, dotting the *I* with a lemon drop (which was rather stale). The others gave her gifts that were thoughtful and mostly handmade:

- A set of Dewey Decimal flash cards from Blythe.

- A book of logic puzzles (stamped DISCARD more than a dozen times, so Dinsy could write in it) from Dorothy.

- A lumpy orange-and-green cardigan Ruth knitted for her.

- A snow globe from the 1939 World's Fair from Olive.

- A flashlight from Edith, so that Dinsy could find her way around at night and not knock over the wastebasket again.

- A set of paper finger puppets, made from blank card pockets, hand-painted by Marian. (They were literary figures, of course, all of them necessarily stout and squarish—Nero Wolfe and Friar Tuck, Santa Claus, and Gertrude Stein.)

But her favorite gift was the second boon she'd wished upon the Library: a box of crayons. (She had grown very tired of drawing gray pictures with the little pencils.) It had produced Crayola crayons, in the familiar yellow-and-green box, labeled LIBRARY PACK. Inside were the colors of Dinsy's world: Reference Maroon, Brown Leather, Peplum Beige, Reader's Guide Green, World Book Red, Card Catalog Cream, Date Stamp Purple, and Palatino Black.

It was a very special birthday, that fourth of July. Although Dinsy wondered about Marian's calculations. As Harriet cut the first piece of cake that evening, she remarked that it was snowing rather heavily outside, which everyone agreed was lovely, but quite unusual for that time of year.

Dinsy soon learned all the planets, and many of their moons. (She referred to herself as Umbriel for an entire month.) She puffed up her cheeks and blew onto stacks of scrap paper. "Sirocco," she'd whisper. "Chinook. Mistral. Willy-Willy," and rated her attempts on the Beaufort scale. Dorothy put a halt to it after Hurricane Dinsy reshuffled a rather elaborate game of Patience.

She dipped into fractals here, double dactyls there. When she tired of a subject—or found it just didn't suit her—Blythe or Dorothy would smile and proffer the hat. It was a deep green felt that held one thousand slips of paper, numbered 001 to 999. Dinsy'd scrunch her eyes closed, pick one, and, like a scavenger hunt, spend the morning (or the next three weeks) at the shelves indicated.

Pangolins lived at 599 (point 31), and Pancakes at 641. Pencils were at 674, but Pens were a shelf away at 681, and Ink was across the aisle at 667. (Dinsy thought that was stupid, because you had to *use* them together.) Pluto the planet was at 523, but Pluto the Disney dog was at 791 (point 453), near Rock and Roll and Kazoos.

It was all very useful information. But in Dinsy's opinion, things could be a little *too* organized.

The first time she straightened up the Common Room without anyone asking, she was very pleased with herself. She had lined up everyone's teacup in a neat row on the shelf, with all the handles curving the same way, and arranged the spices in the little wooden rack: ANISE, BAY LEAVES, CHIVES, DILL WEED, PEPPERCORNS, SALT, SESAME SEEDS, SUGAR.

"Look," she said when Blythe came in to refresh her tea, "Order out of chaos." It was one of Blythe's favorite mottoes.

Blythe smiled and looked over at the spice rack. Then her smile faded and she shook her head.

"Is something wrong?" Dinsy asked. She had hoped for a compliment.

"Well, you used the alphabet," said Blythe, sighing. "I suppose it's not your fault. You were with Olive for a good many years. But you're a big girl now. You should learn the *proper* order." She picked up the salt container. "We'll start with Salt." She wrote the word on the little chalkboard hanging by the icebox, followed by the number 553.632. "Five-five-three-point-six-three-two. Because—?"

Dinsy thought for a moment. "Earth Sciences."

"Ex-actly." Blythe beamed. "Because salt is a mineral. But, now, chives. Chives are a garden crop, so they're…"

Dinsy bit her lip in concentration. "Six-thirty-something."

"Very good." Blythe smiled again and chalked CHIVES 635.26 on the board. "So you see, Chives should always be shelved *after* Salt, dear."

Blythe turned and began to rearrange the eight ceramic jars. Behind her back, Dinsy silently rolled her eyes.

Edith appeared in the doorway.

"Oh, not again," she said. "No wonder I can't find a thing in this kitchen. Blythe, I've *told* you. Bay Leaf comes first. QK-four-nine—" She had worked at the university when she was younger.

"Library of Congress, my fanny," said Blythe, not quite under her breath. "We're not *that* kind of library."

"It's no excuse for imprecision," Edith replied. They each grabbed a jar and stared at each other.

Dinsy tiptoed away and hid in the 814s, where she read "Jabberwocky" until the coast was clear.

But the kitchen remained a taxonomic battleground. At least once a week, Dinsy was amused by the indignant sputtering of someone who had just spooned dill weed, not sugar, into a cup of Earl Grey tea.

Once she knew her way around, Dinsy was free to roam the library as she chose.

"Anywhere?" she asked Blythe.

"Anywhere you like, my sweet. Except the Stacks. You're not quite old enough for the Stacks."

Dinsy frowned. "I am *so,*" she muttered. But the Stacks were locked, and there wasn't much she could do.

Some days she sat with Olive in the Children's Room, revisiting old friends, or explored the maze of the Main Room. Other days she spent in the Reference Room, where Ruth and Harriet guarded the big important books that no one could ever, ever check out—not even when the library had been open.

Ruth and Harriet were like a set of salt-and-pepper shakers from two different yard sales. Harriet had faded orange hair and a sharp, kind face. Small and pinched and pointed, a decade or two away from wizened. She had violet eyes and a mischievous, conspiratorial smile and wore rimless octagonal glasses, like stop signs. Dinsy had never seen an actual stop sign, but she'd looked at pictures.

Ruth was Chinese. She wore wool jumpers in neon plaids and had cat's-eye glasses on a beaded chain around her neck. She never put them all the way on, just lifted them to her eyes and peered through them without opening the bows.

"Life is a treasure hunt," said Harriet.

"Knowledge is power," said Ruth. "Knowing where to look is half the battle."

"Half the fun," added Harriet. Ruth almost never got the last word.

They introduced Dinsy to dictionaries and almanacs, encyclopedias and compendiums. They had been native guides through the country of the Dry Tomes for many years, but they agreed that Dinsy delved unusually deep.

"Would you like to take a break, love?" Ruth asked one afternoon. "It's nearly time for tea."

"I *am* fatigued," Dinsy replied, looking up from *Roget*. "Fagged out, weary, a bit spent. Tea would be pleasant, agreeable—"

"I'll put the kettle on," sighed Ruth.

Dinsy read *Bartlett's* as if it were a catalog of conversations, spouting lines from Tennyson, Mark Twain, and Dale Carnegie until even Harriet put her hands over her ears and began to hum "Stairway to Heaven."

One or two evenings a month, usually after Blythe had remarked "Well, she's a spirited girl," for the third time, they all took the night off, "For Library business." Olive or Dorothy would tuck Dinsy in early and read from one of her favorites while Ruth made her a bedtime treat—a cup of spiced tea that tasted a little like cherries and a little like varnish, and which Dinsy somehow never remembered finishing.

A list (written in diverse hands), tacked to the wall of the Common Room.

<u>10 Things to Remember
When You Live in a Library</u>

1. We do not play shuffleboard on the Reading Room table.

2. Books should not have "dog's ears." Bookmarks make lovely presents.

3. Do not write in books. Even in pencil. Puzzle collections and connect-the-dots are books.

4. The shelving cart is not a scooter.

5. Library paste is not food.
   [Marginal note in a child's hand:
   True. It tastes like Cream of Wrong Soup.]

6. Do not use the date stamp to mark your banana.

7. Shelves are not monkey bars.
8. Do not play 982-pickup with the P-Q drawer (or any other).
9. The dumbwaiter is only for books. It is not a carnival ride.
10. Do not drop volumes of the Britannica off the stairs to hear the echo.

They were an odd, but contented family. There were rules, to be sure, but Dinsy never lacked for attention. With seven mothers, there was always someone to talk with, a hankie for tears, a lap or a shoulder to share a story.

Most evenings, when Dorothy had made a fire in the Reading Room and the wooden shelves gleamed in the flickering light, they would all sit in companionable silence. Ruth knitted, Harriet muttered over an acrostic, Edith stirred the cocoa so it wouldn't get a skin. Dinsy sat on the rug, her back against the knees of whoever was her favorite that week, and felt safe and warm and loved. "God's in his heaven, all's right with the world," as Blythe would say.

But as she watched the moon peep in and out of the clouds through the leaded-glass panes of the tall windows, Dinsy often wondered what it would be like to see the whole sky, all around her.

First Olive and then Dorothy had been in charge of Dinsy's thick dark hair, trimming it with the mending shears every few weeks when it began to obscure her eyes. But a few years into her second decade at the library, Dinsy began cutting it herself, leaving it as wild and spiky as the brambles outside the front door.

That was not the only change.

"We haven't seen her at breakfast in weeks," Harriet said as she buttered a scone one morning.

"Months. And all she reads is Salinger. Or Sylvia Plath," complained Dorothy. "I wouldn't mind that so much, but she just leaves them on the table for *me* to reshelve."

"It's not as bad as what she did to Olive," Marian said. "*The Golden Compass* appeared last week, and she thought Dinsy would enjoy it. But not only did she turn up her nose, she had the gall to say to Olive, 'Leave me alone. I can find my own books.' Imagine. Poor Olive was beside herself."

"She used to be such a sweet child." Blythe sighed. "What are we going to do?"

"Now, now. She's just at that age," Edith said calmly. "She's not really a child anymore. She needs some privacy, and some responsibility. I have an idea."

And so it was that Dinsy got her own room—with a door that *shut*—in a corner of the second floor. It had been a tiny cubbyhole of an office, but it had a set of slender curved stairs, wrought iron worked with lilies and twigs, which led up to the turret between the red-tiled eaves.

The round tower was just wide enough for Dinsy's bed, with windows all around. There had once been a view of the town, but now trees and ivy allowed only jigsaw puzzle–shaped puddles of light to dapple the wooden floor. At night the puddles were luminous blue splotches of moonlight that hinted of magic beyond her reach.

On the desk in the room below, centered in a pool of yellow lamplight, Edith had left a note: "Come visit me. There's mending to be done," and a worn brass key on a wooden paddle, stenciled with the single word: STACKS.

The Stacks were in the basement, behind a locked gate at the foot of the metal spiral staircase that descended from the 600s. They had always reminded Dinsy of the steps down to the dungeon in *The King's Stilts*. Darkness below hinted at danger, but adventure. Terra Incognita.

Dinsy didn't use her key the first day, or the second. Mending? Boring. But the afternoon of the third day, she ventured down the spiral stairs. She had been as far as the gate before, many times, because it was forbidden, to peer through the metal mesh at the dimly lighted shelves and imagine what treasures might be hidden there.

She had thought that the Stacks would be damp and cold, strewn with odd bits of discarded library flotsam. Instead they were cool and dry, and smelled very different from upstairs. Dustier, with hints of mold and the tang of vintage leather, an undertone of vinegar stored in an old shoe.

Unlike the main floor, with its polished wood and airy high ceilings, the Stacks were a low, cramped warren of gunmetal gray shelves that ran floor to ceiling in narrow aisles. Seven levels twisted behind the west wall of the library like a secret labyrinth that stretched from below the ground to up under the eaves of the roof. Floor and steps were translucent glass brick and six-foot ceilings strung with pipes and ducts were lit by single caged bulbs, two to an aisle.

It was a windowless fortress of books. Upstairs the shelves were mosaics of all colors and sizes, but the Stacks were filled with geometric monochrome blocks of subdued colors: eight dozen forest-green bound volumes of *Ladies' Home Journal* filled five rows of shelves, followed by an equally large block of identical dark red *LIFE*s.

Dinsy felt like she was in another world. She was not lost, but for the first time in her life, she was not easily found, and that suited her. She could sit, invisible, and listen to the sounds of library life going on around her. From Level Three she could hear Ruth humming in the Reference Room on the other side of the wall. Four feet away, and it felt like miles. She wandered and browsed for a month before she presented herself at Edith's office.

A frosted glass pane in the dark wood door said MENDING ROOM in chipping gold letters. The door was open a few inches, and Dinsy could see a long workbench strewn with sewn folios and bits of leather bindings, spools of thread, and bottles of thick beige glue.

"I gather you're finding your way around," Edith said, without turning in her chair. "I haven't had to send out a search party."

"Pretty much," Dinsy replied. "I've been reading old magazines." She flopped into a chair to the left of the door.

"One of my favorite things," Edith agreed. "It's like time travel." Edith was a tall, solid woman with long graying hair that she wove into elaborate buns and twisted braids, secured with number-two pencils and a single tortoiseshell comb. She wore blue jeans and vests in brightly muted colors—pale teal and lavender and dusky rose—with a strand of lapis lazuli beads cut in rough ovals.

Edith repaired damaged books, a job that was less demanding now that nothing left the building. But some of the bound volumes of journals and abstracts and magazines went back as far as 1870, and their leather bindings were crumbling into dust. The first year, Dinsy's job was to go through the aisles, level by level, and find the volumes that needed the most help. Edith gave her a clipboard and told her to check in now and then.

Dinsy learned how to take apart old books and put them back together again. Her first mending project was the tattered 1877 volume of *American Naturalist*, with its articles on

"Educated Fleas" and "Barnacles" and "The Cricket as Thermometer." She sewed pages into signatures, trimmed leather, and marbleized paper. Edith let her make whatever she wanted out of the scraps, and that year Dinsy gave everyone miniature replicas of their favorite volumes for Christmas.

She liked the craft, liked doing something with her hands. It took patience and concentration, and that was oddly soothing. After supper, she and Edith often sat and talked for hours, late into the night, mugs of cocoa on their workbenches, the rest of the library dark and silent above them.

"What's it like outside?" Dinsy asked one night while she was waiting for some glue to dry.

Edith was silent for a long time, long enough that Dinsy wondered if she'd spoken too softly, and was about to repeat the question, when Edith replied.

"Chaos."

That was not anything Dinsy had expected. "What do you mean?"

"It's noisy. It's crowded. Everything's always changing, and not in any way you can predict."

"That sounds kind of exciting," Dinsy said.

"Hmm." Edith thought for a moment. "Yes, I suppose it could be."

Dinsy mulled that over and fiddled with a scrap of leather, twisting it in her fingers before she spoke again. "Do you ever miss it?"

Edith turned on her stool and looked at Dinsy. "Not often," she said slowly. "Not as often as I'd thought. But then I'm awfully fond of order. Fonder than most, I suppose. This is a better fit."

Dinsy nodded and took a sip of her cocoa.

A few months later, she asked the Library for a third and final boon.

The evening that everything changed, Dinsy sat in the armchair in her room, reading Trollope's *Can You Forgive Her?* (for the third time), imagining what it would be like to talk to Glencora, when a tentative knock sounded at the door.

"Dinsy? Dinsy?" said a tiny familiar voice. "It's Olive, dear."

Dinsy slid her READ! bookmark into chapter 14 and closed the book. "It's open," she called.

Olive padded in wearing a red flannel robe, her feet in worn carpet slippers. Dinsy expected her to proffer a book, but instead Olive said, "I'd like you to come with me, dear." Her blue eyes shone with excitement.

"What for?" They had all done a nice reading of *As You Like It* a few days before, but Dinsy didn't remember any plans for that night. Maybe Olive just wanted company. Dinsy had been meaning to spend an evening in the Children's Room, but hadn't made it down there in months.

But Olive surprised her. "It's Library business," she said, waggling her finger, but smiling.

Now, that was intriguing. For years, whenever the Librarians wanted an evening to themselves, they'd disappear down into the Stacks after supper, and would never tell her why. "It's Library business," was all they ever said. When she was younger, Dinsy had tried to follow them, but it's hard to sneak in a quiet place. She was always caught and given that awful cherry tea. The next thing she knew it was morning.

"Library business?" Dinsy said slowly. "And I'm invited?"

"Yes, dear. You're practically all grown up now. It's high time you joined us."

"Great." Dinsy shrugged, as if it were no big deal, trying to hide her excitement. And maybe it wasn't a big deal. Maybe it was a meeting of the rules committee, or plans for moving the 340s to the other side of the window again. But what if it *was* something special…? That was both exciting and a little scary.

She wiggled her feet into her own slippers and stood up. Olive barely came to her knees. Dinsy touched the old woman's white hair affectionately, remembering when she used to snuggle into that soft lap. Such a long time ago.

A library at night is a still but resonant place. The only lights were the sconces along the walls, and Dinsy could hear the faint echo of each footfall on the stairs down to the foyer. They walked through the shadows of the shelves in the Main Room, back to the 600s, and down the metal stairs to the Stacks, footsteps ringing hollowly.

The lower level was dark except for a single caged bulb above the rows of *National Geographic*s, their yellow bindings pale against the gloom. Olive turned to the left.

"Where are we going?" Dinsy asked. It was so odd to be down there with Olive.

"You'll see," Olive said. Dinsy could practically feel her smiling in the dark. "You'll see."

She led Dinsy down an aisle of boring municipal reports and stopped at the far end, in front of the door to the janitorial closet set into the stone wall. She pulled a long, old-fashioned brass key from the pocket of her robe and handed it to Dinsy.

"You open it, dear. The keyhole's a bit high for me."

Dinsy stared at the key, at the door, back at the key. She'd been fantasizing about "Library Business" since she was little, imagining all sorts of scenarios, none of them involving cleaning supplies. A monthly poker game. A secret tunnel into town, where they all went dancing, like the twelve princesses. Or a book group, reading forbidden texts. And now they were inviting her in? What a letdown if it was just maintenance.

She put the key in the lock. "Funny," she said as she turned it. "I've always wondered what went on when you—" Her voice caught in her throat. The door opened, not onto the closet of mops and pails and bottles of Pine-Sol she expected, but onto a small room, paneled in wood the color of ancient honey. An Oriental rug in rich, deep reds lay on the parquet floor, and the room shone with the light of dozens of candles. There were no shelves, no books, just a small fireplace at one end where a log crackled in the hearth.

"Surprise," said Olive softly. She gently tugged Dinsy inside.

All the others were waiting, dressed in flowing robes of different colors. Each of them stood in front of a Craftsman rocker, dark wood covered in soft brown leather.

Edith stepped forward and took Dinsy's hand. She gave it a gentle squeeze and said, under her breath, "Don't worry." Then she winked and led Dinsy to an empty rocker. "Stand here," she said, and returned to her own seat.

Stunned, Dinsy stood, her mouth open, her feelings a kaleidoscope.

"Welcome, dear one," said Dorothy. "We'd like you to join us." Her face was serious, but her eyes were bright, as if she was about to tell a really awful riddle and couldn't wait for the reaction.

Dinsy started. That was almost word for word what Olive had said, and it made her nervous. She wasn't sure what was coming, and was even less sure that she was ready.

"Introductions first." Dorothy closed her eyes and intoned, "I am Lexica. I serve the Library." She bowed her head once and sat down.

Dinsy stared, her eyes wide and her mind reeling as each of the librarians repeated what was obviously a familiar rite.

"I am Juvenilia," said Olive with a twinkle. "I serve the Library."

"Incunabula," said Edith.

"Sapientia," said Harriet.

"Ephemera," said Marian.

"Marginalia," said Ruth.

"Melvilia," said Blythe, smiling at Dinsy. "And I, too, serve the Library."

And then they were all seated, and all looking up at Dinsy.

"How old are you now, my sweet?" asked Harriet.

Dinsy frowned. It wasn't as easy a question as it sounded. "Seventeen," she said after a few seconds. "Or close enough."

"No longer a child." Harriet nodded. There was a touch of sadness in her voice. "That is why we are here tonight. To ask you to join us."

There was something so solemn in Harriet's voice that it made Dinsy's stomach knot up. "I don't understand," she said slowly. "What do you mean? I've been here my whole life. Practically."

Dorothy shook her head. "You have been *in* the Library, but not *of* the Library. Think of it as an apprenticeship. We have nothing more to teach you. So we're asking if you'll take a Library name and truly become one of us. There have always been seven to serve the Library."

Dinsy looked around the room. "Won't I be the eighth?" she asked. She was curious, but she was also stalling for time.

"No, dear," said Olive. "You'll be taking my place. I'm retiring. I can barely reach the second shelves these days, and soon I'll be no bigger than the dictionary. I'm going to put my feet up and sit by the fire and take it easy. I've earned it," she said with a decisive nod.

"Here, here," said Blythe. "And well done, too."

There was a murmur of assent around the room.

Dinsy took a deep breath, and then another. She looked around the room at the eager faces of the seven librarians, the only mothers she had ever known. She loved them all, and was about to disappoint them, because she had a secret of her own. She closed her eyes so she wouldn't see their faces, not at first.

"I can't take your place, Olive," she said quietly, and heard the tremor in her own voice as she fought back tears.

All around her the librarians clucked in surprise. Ruth recovered first. "Well, of course not. No one's asking you to *replace* Olive, we're merely—"

"I can't join you," Dinsy repeated. Her voice was just as quiet, but it was stronger. "Not now."

"But why *not*, sweetie?" That was Blythe, who sounded as if she were about to cry herself.

"Fireworks," said Dinsy after a moment. She opened her eyes. "Six-sixty-two-point-one." She smiled at Blythe. "I know everything about them. But I've never *seen* any." She looked from face to face again.

"I've never petted a dog or ridden a bicycle or watched the sun rise over the ocean," she said, her voice gaining courage. "I want to feel the wind and eat an ice-cream cone at a carnival. I want to smell jasmine on a spring night and hear an orchestra. I want—" She faltered, and then continued, "I want the chance to dance with a boy."

She turned to Dorothy. "You said you have nothing left to teach me. Maybe that's true. I've learned from each of you that there's nothing in the world I can't discover and explore for myself in these books. Except the world," she added in a whisper. She felt her eyes fill with tears. "You chose the Library. I can't do that without knowing what else there might be."

"You're *leaving*?" Ruth asked in a choked voice.

Dinsy bit her lip and nodded. "I'm, well, I've—" She'd been practicing these words for days, but they were so much harder than she'd thought. She looked down at her hands.

And then Marian rescued her.

"Dinsy's going to college," she said. "Just like I did. And you, and you, and you." She pointed a finger at each of the women in the room. "We were girls before we were librarians, remember? It's her turn now."

"But how—?" asked Edith.

"Where did—?" stammered Harriet.

"I wished on the Library," said Dinsy. "And it left an application in the *Unabridged*. Marian helped me fill it out."

"I *am* in charge of circulation," said Marian. "What comes in, what goes out. We found her acceptance letter in the book return last week."

"But you had no transcripts," said Dorothy practically. "Where did you tell them you'd gone to school?"

Dinsy smiled. "That was Marian's idea. We told them I was home-schooled, raised by feral librarians."

And so it was that on a bright September morning, for the first time in ages, the heavy oak door of the Carnegie Library swung open. Everyone stood in the doorway, blinking in the sunlight.

"Promise you'll write," said Blythe, tucking a packet of sweets into the basket on Dinsy's arm.

The others nodded. "Yes, do."

"I'll try," she said. "But you never know how long *any*thing will take around here." She tried to make a joke of it, but she was holding back tears and her heart was hammering a mile a minute.

"You will come back, won't you? I can't put off my retirement forever." Olive was perched on top of the Circulation Desk.

"To visit, yes." Dinsy leaned over and kissed her cheek. "I promise. But to serve? I don't know. I have no idea what I'm going to find out there." She looked out into the forest that surrounded the library. "I don't even know if I'll be able to get back in, through all that."

"Take this," said Marian. She handed Dinsy a small stiff pasteboard card with a metal plate in one corner, embossed with her name: DINSY CARNEGIE.

"What is it?" asked Dinsy.

"Your library card. It will always get you in."

There were hugs all around, and tears and good-byes. But in the end, the seven librarians stood back and watched her go.

Dinsy stepped out into the world as she had come—with a wicker basket and a book of fairy tales, full of hopes and dreams.

AUTHOR'S NOTE

This story came bubbling up from the Well of Ideas from a couple of different sources.

During a psychic reading about ten years ago (a birthday gift from my sister), I was told that my spirit guides were seven librarians, who would help me find the answers to the questions in my life. I'm not sure I believed that, but I liked the idea, because the library was my favorite refuge, and there have been many significant librarians in my life.

I have always lived with and around books. There was a battered, blue buckram–bound copy of *Heidi* on the bookshelf in the upstairs hall of the house I grew up in. Old book, with nice color plates, dating back to my mother's childhood.

When I was about eight I discovered that *Heidi* had a library-card pocket inside the cover. Overdue library books were a capital crime in my family, and this one had been checked out in 1933, when my mother would have been eight herself. I asked her about it, and to my surprise, she looked embarrassed and said, in a determined but apologetic voice, "I *am* going to return it."

She had checked it out of the Bristow, Oklahoma, library, and her family had moved out of the state two weeks later. It had gotten packed by mistake. She'd been carting it around, from house to house, to college, into her marriage, feeling guilty about it for decades.

Sometime in the mid-1970s, she and a friend were planning a road trip, and Mom looked at the map and realized that if they made a 150-mile detour (each way), they could stop in Bristow. So that summer, my mother marched up the steps of the Bristow Public Library, plunked *Heidi* down on the circulation desk, and said, "This is overdue." An understatement. It was more than *forty years* overdue.

The librarian looked at the book, looked at my mother.

"I'll pay the fine, whatever it is." Mom pulled out her checkbook.

"That won't be necessary," the librarian said. Then she got her DISCARD stamp and whacked *Heidi* and handed the book back.

It's sitting on my desk as I type this.

Eventually, my guiding librarians picked up *Heidi* and wandered into my brain again. They puttered around in there for months before the story began to gel. I wrote most of the first draft in a little cottage in the desert outside Tucson, with downloaded photos of old libraries on my laptop. When I got home, the manuscript and I visited a dozen old Carnegie libraries in northern Ohio, where I sat and wrote and looked at old wooden wainscoting and Craftsman-tiled fireplaces and pebbled-glass office doors. I spent a week sitting on the floor of the stacks in a Case Western Reserve University library, making notes about the smells and the textures so that I could give them to Dinsy.

A Carnegie library is a library built with money donated by Scottish-American businessman and philanthropist Andrew Carnegie. 2,509 Carnegie libraries were built between 1883 and 1929, including some belonging to public and university library systems. 1,689 were built in the United States, 660 in Britain and Ireland, 125 in Canada, and others in Australia, New Zealand, Serbia, the Caribbean, and Fiji. Few towns that requested a grant and agreed to his terms were refused. When the last grant was made in 1919, there were 3,500 libraries in the United States, nearly half of them built with construction grants paid by Carnegie.

(http://en.wikipedia.org/wiki/Carnegie_library)

Illustrations of Carnegie Libraries

Page	Location
ii	Chanute, KS (author's collection)
vi	Braddock, PA (first Carnegie Library in the USA)
5	Olney, IL (author's collection)
10	Cheyney University, Cheyney, PA
18	Children's Reading Room, Bexley, OH (author's collection)
22	Crawfordsville, IN
27	Ballard Branch, Seattle, WA
31	Hamilton, OH
37	Greenlake Branch, Seattle, WA
42	Fond du Lac, WI
49	Hayward, CA
68	Mt. Vernon, IL
71	University Branch, Seattle, WA
76	Norwalk, OH
77	Parsons, KS

Seattle, WA, images courtesy Gerry Gillmore.
All others from public domain sources.

Biography

ELLEN KLAGES is the author of the short story collection, *Portable Childhoods*, and two acclaimed YA novels: *The Green Glass Sea*, which won the Scott O'Dell Award, the New Mexico Book Award, and the Lopez Award; and *White Sands, Red Menace*, which won the California and New Mexico Book awards. Her short stories have been have been translated into Czech, French, German, Hungarian, Japanese, and Swedish, and have been nominated for the Nebula Award, the Hugo, World Fantasy, and Campbell awards. Her story, "Basement Magic," won a Nebula in 2005. She lives in San Francisco, in a small house full of strange and wondrous things.